D0602291

For João and Gabriela.

First published in the United States in 2018 by
Eerdmans Books for Young Readers,
an imprint of Wm. B. Eerdmans Publishing Co.
2140 Oak Industrial Dr. NE, Grand Rapids, Michigan 49505
www.eerdmans.com/youngreaders

Text and illustrations © Renato Moriconi
Originally published in Brazil by Companhia das Letrinhas under the title *Bárbaro*.
English-language edition © 2018 Eerdmans Books for Young Readers
Published by arrangement with Debbie Bibo Agency

Manufactured in China

27 26 25 24 23 22 21 20 19 18   1 2 3 4 5 6 7 8 9

ISBN 978-0-8028-5509-1

A catalog record of this book is available from the Library of Congress.

THE LITTLE BARBARIAN

Renato Moriconi

Eerdmans Books for Young Readers

Grand Rapids, Michigan

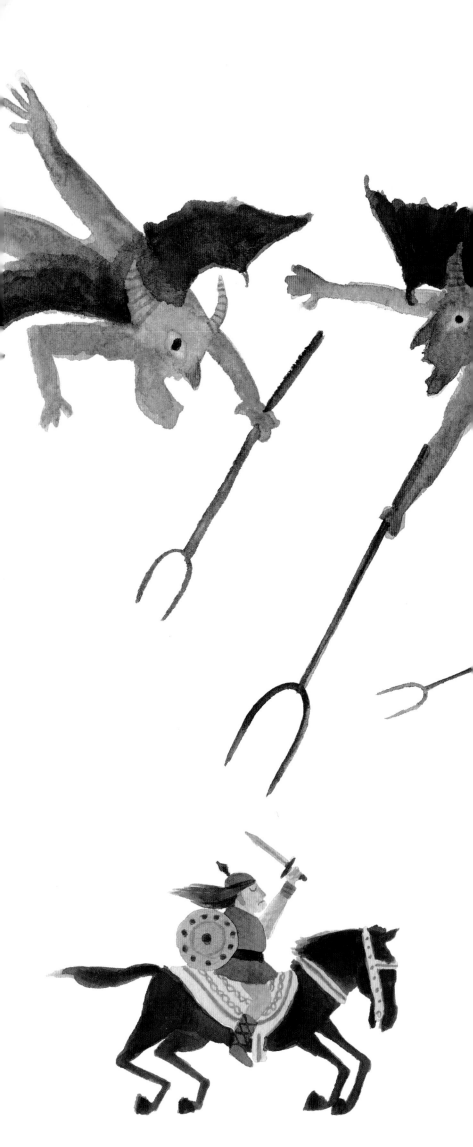

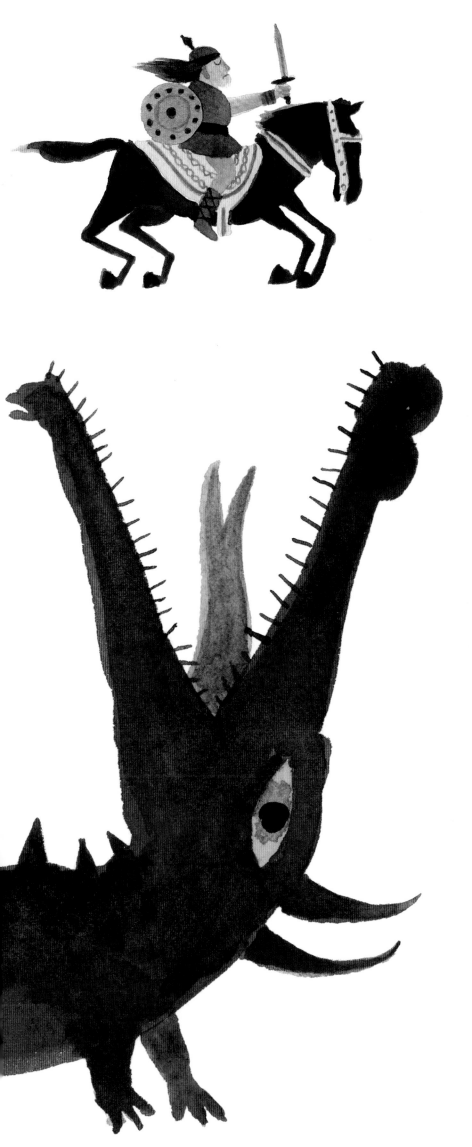

Renato Moriconi is a Brazilian writer and visual artist. He doesn't currently ride carousels, because his wife says he's too big for that. He plans to move to Asgard and become a barbarian with a beautiful shield and a sword for fighting monsters and other dangerous creatures (if his wife lets him, of course).

Renato has had more than fifty books for children published in a number of countries throughout the world. The Brazilian edition of *The Little Barbarian* received many prizes, including the FNLIJ award for Best Wordless Picture Book and the prestigious Jabuti Award for Best Children's Illustration.